MW00948158

LAUGHABLE LEGENDS OF MIDDLE SCHOOL 99

VOL. 1

DAVID PARIS

Illustrations by

Andrea Vitali & Joe Shepherd

ISBN-13: 978-1976581762
ISBN-10: 1976581761

CONTENTS

ACKNOWLEDGMENTS

I want to thank my best friend, Zoë Klein, for believing in me and supporting me. This book would never have happened without your feedback, technical assistance, and enthusiasm. I want to thank all of my students, who are the inspiration for these stories. Big thanks to my brother Ben, who has been an advocate of all my artistic pursuits throughout my life. Thank you to my roommate Josie for listening to all the stories, sharing with me what worked, and giving me suggestions for what did not work. Thank you to the teachers of M.S. 88 for your contributions, especially Mr. Rosensweig, Ms. Wolfe, and Mr. Walling. Thank you to Andrea and Joe for such incredible illustrations, bringing another dimension to the stories. Thank you, Athena, for reminding me about the power and importance of story. And thank you to my ancestral spirit for your guidance and protection as I try to fulfill that promise to make the world a better place.

ABOUT THE BOOK

I am a middle school literacy teacher in the heart of my hometown in Brooklyn, New York. For most of my students, reading was a chore and held no value in their lives. For twenty years, I have battled video games, hormones, and gossip in and out of the classroom. In order to build a connection to literacy, I often told "true" stories about school legends that were obviously *not* true. This was the only time I had the full attention of the class. These stories explained what seemed to be the hot topics on the minds of every middle school student: conflict, acceptance, visibility, and power. Through outrageous depictions of absurdity, these stories aimed to address these important issues and inspire dialogue. Bullying was portrayed in one story "Why Do Bullies Get Pimples on Their Noses?" The problems of peer pressure were brought to life by the story "The Boy Who Cared and the Boy Who Didn't." And the destructive issue of gossip was addressed in "The Worst Kind of Ghost." The stories were fast, fun, and often fantastical. Students laughed together, shared common experiences, and built a connection that helped create a positive classroom community.

Laughable Legends at Middle School 99 is my attempt to build on those magical moments and create more conversations about middle school life. The stories are edgy and based on real-life situations in order to spark authentic participation and bypass pretense. There can be immense healing when kids learn that they are not alone about what they think and feel, especially in middle school. When students talk about their experiences, they feel safer, more expressive, and more comfortable showing themselves. I have included discussion questions in the appendix to help in this process. It is my hope that the book is one vehicle that can help create the space for laughter, recognition, and reflection. And if kids connect to the power of stories and reading, that is a bonus.

INTRODUCTION

Middle school is a crazy place. Why are teachers so cranky? Why are some kids mean on Thursdays but not Mondays? Why do adults try to fix problems and only make the situation worse? I try to answer these questions by telling stories and legends that explain life today. These stories are based on my own experiences as a student as well as a middle school teacher. I hope the stories are entertaining and inspire you to share your experience about what it's like to be a middle school student. Please visit www.middleschoollifeskills.com to share your own stories and laughable legends.

PART I

Illustrations

by

Andre Vitali

1
EIGHTH GRADE WILL BE THE BEST THREE YEARS OF YOUR LIFE

Students are threatened every year that they better do their work or they won't graduate. It is an empty threat that gets twenty-three seconds of respect. After that, students return to gossiping, daydreaming, or whistling pop songs to no one in particular. There is a reason these threats never become reality. And that reason is Charlie Humphries.

Twenty-three years ago, Charlie failed every class on his report card, failed to show his report card to his parents, and failed to care about failing. What no adult understood is that Charlie loved Middle School 99. He loved spending two hours' detention after school. He loved his punishments before school. He even loved summer school. When Charlie failed, he actually succeeded. Because of his odd version of love, Charlie managed to spend more time at Middle School 99 than any student in history. And his method was failure.

Charlie managed to get a −10 on his spelling test. He would only write about the future in history class. His science labs would explode. His algebra was poetic, and his poetry assignments solved algebraic equations. In gym,

he would sing, and in drama class, he would wrestle. Charlie was brilliant in getting the lowest possible grades in every possible subject.

Charlie was also smart about getting in trouble. He once brought a water pistol to class. Most troublemakers would simply shoot it at people, but Charlie was special. He sat in the back of class and shot the ceiling. That way, when the water dripped on the students, they thought the

ceiling was collapsing. Every day the custodian would inspect and swear that nothing was wrong. And every day, Charlie would find a new spot to create a phantom leak. He was never caught until he took a selfie with the water pistol, and posted it on the principal's door. When he got five hours of detention, he celebrated quietly, looking at the ceiling with great pride, joy, and belonging. He loved Middle School 99.

Charlie was brilliant, and he successfully repeated the eighth grade two times. Something different needed to happen for a kid who loved punishment. The school psychologist, Dr. Kerensky, was called into the school to observe Charlie. Dr. Kerensky watched Charlie's health class learn about meditation.

Everyone knew Charlie was going to ruin the lesson, but to everyone's surprise, Charlie was quiet. The health teacher, Ms. Lester, challenged the students to see if they could match her inner stillness, her unique calmness of mind, by not moving or talking. What no one knew is that Charlie hid a remote-control fart machine in her seat cushion! He had the remote in his palm, and he was determined to challenge the Zen mind of Middle School 99's health teacher.

The first fart sound was a light squeeze of wind that clearly came from underneath Ms. Lester's butt. To Ms. Lester's credit, she didn't move or say a thing, but her nose did sniffle in curiosity. After one minute of controlled silence, Charlie pressed the green button firmly. This released a stronger plush sound that was impossible to ignore, and the students either snickered or laughed or inched away because they were afraid of the smell. Even Mr. Kerensky wondered what Ms. Lester had for lunch.

Ms. Lester could not stay in her meditative pose and had to react to the accusatory eyes. She told the class not to be rude, as she circled five times around her seat cushion trying to figure out where the sound came from. She even lifted the cushion but could not find the source of the mysterious sound. She too thought that maybe her lunch was too gaseous, or maybe she was getting too old to control her butt. Either way, she returned to her seat, settled the class down, and was determined to teach the value of meditation. She was also thankful that the fart did not smell.

4

Unfortunately for Ms. Lester, there was a red button on the remote. Charlie hesitated for a moment, because the instruction manual stated that the red button was only for emergency revenge scenarios. But it was too tempting. Just as Ms. Lester fell into a peaceful position, he pressed the button as hard as he could, and the explosion was amazing. It was the wettest, nastiest fart you have ever heard, with bonus sounds of diarrhea. The reaction was even more impressive. Not only did Ms. Lester scream—she ran. And not only did the class follow her, but they also mimicked her fart as they chased her down the hallway. Charlie left the remote on Ms. Lester's desk, made sure his initials were visible on the back cover, and gave Mr. Kerensky a look of triumph. Massive detention would be coming his way.

To Charlie's surprise and disappointment, he was not punished, but he was praised for his prank. Teachers gave him high fives because Ms. Lester was considered a snob and needed a humbling experience. Charlie thought this was an odd response, but he didn't think it was suspicious until he received a letter of commendation for falsely pulling the fire alarm. The certificate said that he was commended for thinking ahead and preparing the school for an emergency. He absolutely knew something was wrong when his picture of stealing a computer was on a green wall devoted to recycling unused materials. What was happening?

Charlie remembered that the consequences of his mischievousness changed the day Mr. Kerensky showed up to observe him. Charlie went to the psychologist's office and demanded the truth. Mr. Kerensky was transparent, explained everything, and gave Charlie the worst possible news. No matter what he did, Charlie was going to graduate. Charlie felt defeated. He pleaded for more detention, more punishments, more parent conferences, and more tests to fail. But it was too late. He had to admit he was scared to leave middle school. He didn't want to start all over again in a new school, but he had no choice. Charlie failed for the first time in his life, by not being able to fail.

Charlie graduated and is no longer a student at Middle School 99, but his presence is everywhere. Whenever a teacher gets weak with consequences, a dean gets soft with punishments, or a principal gets forgiving, they are probably thinking that you might be failing on purpose. Never mistake their true motivation. It is not kindness. It is not caring. They are scared of Charlie Humphries. You can thank him anytime. And, oh yeah, if you ever farted but really didn't fart, do not get scared. That's the revenge of Ms. Lester's ghost, whose presence also can sometimes be felt, smelled, and definitely heard. She is still looking for Charlie Humphries and always will be.

2

THE GIRL WHO LOVED CIRCLES

Nobody likes to get in a line, but you would be surprised to know why. Forty-two years ago at Middle School 99, Ophelia stood out for loving circles. She always wore clothes with polka dots. Ophelia liked the words "oops" and "booboos." She had Cheerios for breakfast, Oreos for lunch, and SpaghettiOs for dinner. She came to school early so that she could circle around the school. She used a hole puncher whenever she could and loved sprinkling the paper circles over her head. Whenever she took the bus, she always sang, "The wheels on the bus go 'round and 'round, 'round and 'round…"

School life often supported Ophelia's passion for

circles. She thought Venn diagrams were masterpieces of art. She was mesmerized by the spinning globe in geography class. In gym class, she loved soccer, Hula Hoops, and Frisbees, although she never threw or kicked anything in a straight line. Ophelia brought her own paper plates to lunch because she hated rectangular trays.

Sometimes, life at school was tough for Ophelia. She refused to look at any corners in a room. She would protest anytime x beat o in ticktacktoe. She cried whenever a pizza pie was sliced. And worst of all, the geometry teacher once demanded that she ruin a circle by drawing a radius. Surprisingly, there was another student, Lionel, who made the tough times bearable.

Lionel loved lines. He woke up every morning excited by waiting in a line for a bagel. Lionel walked in one direction to school, even if it meant walking through someone's house or even traffic in the street. Lionel loved wearing stripes, writing timelines, and staring at the beauty of lined paper and was ecstatic over graph paper.

Astonishingly, Lionel always knew what to say to Ophelia. He told her that if you went in a straight line around the world, you would make a circle. He talked about using straight bars of steel to build Ferris wheels and merry-go-rounds. He told her that politicians pretend to be straight talkers but actually talk in circles. And when life at Middle School 99 felt incomplete to Ophelia, Lionel spray-painted the school sign, so there were four circles, "Middle School 88."

Ophelia and Lionel's friendship was not perfect, and they argued at times. However, Ophelia could never stay mad at Lionel because Lionel always said, "Sooooo sooooory!" He would give her flowers, and she would cut the stem to make the flowers rounder. To no one's surprise, the relationship turned romantic.

On a full moon in October, they had their first date.

Ophelia arrived at a barbecue restaurant on a unicycle and Lionel used a zip line. For dinner, Ophelia ordered a hamburger, and Lionel decided on a hot dog. When dessert was served, they split a cupcake in the most unusual way. Ophelia took a knife and cut the cupcake into a square. Lionel smiled and then shaped what was left into a circle. This thoughtful division continued until unfortunately there was nothing left, except a lot of laughter.

They decided to take a walk to look at the stars. While Ophelia admired the circular planets and stars, Lionel appreciated the constellations that connected them. They held hands as Lionel walked in a straight line and Ophelia walked in a circle around him. As they approached the top of a hill, Ophelia stared into Lionel's round eyes, while Lionel looked at Ophelia's straight nose. Their lips met like magnets, and the world was forever transformed.

Suddenly, ice cream lovers didn't have to feel bad about not liking pie or cake. Dog lovers stopped arguing that cat lovers were weird. Apple juice fanatics let orange juice lovers drink in peace. And best of all, adults let kids be kids.

Ophelia and Lionel's first date turned into a partnership for life, and their love still affects people today. Do you know that moment in an argument when you don't hate the other person for having a different opinion, when you can agree to disagree? You can thank the love Ophelia and Lionel had for each other. You can see that energy every day when some kids line up and some kids refuse to get in line. And if you look closely, Lionel is standing with those in line, while Ophelia is with those students who hate lines, dancing in circles.

3

THE BOY WHO CARED AND THE BOY WHO DIDN'T

Angel Domingo was the kindest kid Middle School 99 ever had. Seventeen years ago, he created his own lost and found for broken hearts. He whistled warnings when bullies were on a warpath. His handshakes could last for two minutes, and his hugs could last two days. He complimented everyone on his or her appearance, even those students who appeared to not care about their appearance.

Many people were baffled by Angel's behavior. He clapped sincerely whenever his teacher remembered his name. Upon a refreshing sip of water, Angel gave thanks to the many men and women who built pipes to bring water to the water fountain. Angel played traffic cop in the hallways and even gave out tickets. And if there was a fight, he would distract the students until they calmed down or until he could trap them in a closet.

Angel's positivity inspired a reaction in everyone. Some were inspired to be kind, but others were inspired to feel spiteful, irritated, and dismissive. Damian Batton was in the last group and felt all three of these emotions, which was unusual because Damian worked very hard to not feel anything at all. Damian realized very early in his middle school life that you were cool if you pretended not to care and you insulted those kids who did care. Insult my face? Doesn't bother me. By the way, your face looks like a minefield. Bad grades? I don't care. You're a nerd. I slip on

the floor, drop my soda on my pants, and get mustard on my face? No big deal. Look at that other loser!

Unfortunately for Damian, Angel was making kindness cool and popular. The Random Acts of Kindness club placed candy bars under seats in the math class and gave out donuts at lunch. The Pay It Forward club lent people money with an unlimited time for reimbursement and no paperwork. The Inclusion club made sure no one sat alone, stood alone, and even felt alone. Damian found that his detachment made him a target of attention and that his insults were drowned out by appreciations. This was not acceptable!

Damian took out a book from the library about being cool and retreated to an isolated corner of the boy's bathroom. The first chapter had only a title and no other words. The title read, "It's Not Cool to Read." The second chapter also had no words except for the title. It read, "Stop Trying So Hard, It's Not Cool." The title of the third chapter  was, "Stop Being So Desperate, Seriously." Only when Damian reached chapter ten, did he find the information he needed. The title of chapter ten read, "Make People Afraid of Difference." Damian knew exactly what to do.

Damian started labeling acts of kindness as weird and looked down on anyone who was nice, even if he or she was taller than him. He encouraged people to not hang out with students who acted differently. Sadly, this dismissive energy attracted some students and scared others. It became a contagious disease unleashed to fight students who cared, and the results were powerful. Many students were afraid to be enthusiastic because they didn't want to be labeled dramatic. Students were afraid to express happiness over their success because they feared they would be perceived as bragging. Worst of all, no one even dared to fight back, or they would be outsiders. No one dared, except Angel Domingo.

Angel still walked around with a hand truck to ship people's book bags from one class to another. Angel loved hopping around the hallways, giving out rainbow colored hard-boiled eggs for Easter. He wore superhero costumes and encouraged others to join him for the good of the world. Some kids followed his lead, but unfortunately, many did not.

Angel and Damian's battle over whether to care or not care is a timeless struggle that still exists today. It is often fought every period in every classroom. It is the essential middle school student's dilemma. How can we be who we want to be, and how do we face the people who might not accept us for who we are? In these times, remember Angel Domingo. He is still around, always happy, ready to lend a helping hand.

4

THE GRAFFITI WRITER

A blank page. A blank wall. A blank expression. Carl couldn't help himself. He had to write his name on anything blank. He used a marker, spray paint, ketchup, or whatever was available. He wanted to be known on page twenty-five of the sixth-grade math textbook, underneath the water fountain, and even on the morning announcements. He loved being famous. And twenty-five years ago, he had written his famous signature all over Middle School 99.

Mr. Clemmons had nightmares of Carl's graffiti. He was the school custodian who had to paint over Carl's name on the bathroom wall, the school's front door, and even the ceiling in the auditorium. Mr. Clemmons devised a plan to cure Carl of his cravings. He brought him to the art room for the first three hours of the school day to exhaust all of his tagging energy. After 1,239 signatures, a very sore wrist, and twenty boxes of spray paint, Mr. Clemmons thought Carl had worn out his urge to write graffiti. But on the way out, Carl sprayed-painted "Thank you" on the door and included his signature.

It was time for plan B. After Carl wrote his name on a wall, Mr. Clemmons would write other kid's names next to, below and above Carl's name. Mr. Clemmons thought that if Carl's name was not special anymore, if his name was surrounded by other names, then maybe he wouldn't write anymore graffiti. Unfortunately, Carl had the opposite reaction. He felt even more special. Carl thought that he inspired a graffiti revolution. And even worse, now Mr. Clemmons had even more names to clean off the walls.

It was time for plan C. Mr. Clemmons thought that if Carl could appreciate the beauty of open space, he might be cured of his destructive habit. One day after school, Mr. Clemmons brought Carl to the roof to appreciate the clear sky. Unfortunately, Carl saw the sky as a canvas and daydreamed about skywriting his name with a small plane. Mr. Clemmons tried again by bringing Carl out to the open air of the baseball field, but Carl never looked up. He was writing his name in the sand in front of home plate.

Plan D had to resort to old-school punishment. Mr. Clemmons decided that Carl needed to clean his own graffiti after school, while listening to opera and using a toothbrush! If Carl could connect the pain to his graffiti, maybe he would think twice. When Carl was finished with three hours of scrubbing, Mr. Clemmons asked him what he learned from his punishment. Carl responded, "I will never run out of places I can write graffiti. I can clean any old tag and replace it with a fresh new signature the next day!"

It was time for a home visit. Mr. Clemmons needed to investigate Carl's background and find out the root of the problem. When Mr. Clemmons arrived, he expected to find Carl's home full of graffiti, but the opposite was true. Carl lived in an immaculate, orderly house without any graffiti. The walls were all white and blank, there were no art supplies, and you couldn't find any evidence of Carl anywhere. And that is how Mr. Clemmons finally realized how to solve Carl's graffiti problem. Graffiti was a strategy to be known. Carl just wanted people to respect him for whom he was. Mr. Clemmons just needed Carl to change his strategy.

The next day, Carl found a megaphone in his locker with a note that read, "So everyone will know who you are." And as instructed in the note, whenever Carl felt compelled to write his name on a wall, he yelled in the megaphone instead. Eighty-three times that day, Carl announced to everyone his name, and instantly Mr. Clemmons had less work to do. There was just a new small problem, but nothing someone else couldn't clean up.

5

THE GAS PROBLEM

Middle School 99 has historically tried to be environmentally friendly. Forty-one years ago, they failed. Most called the failure "air pollution." Some called it "noise pollution." Either way, there was a lot of pollution caused by a fart problem. It was called "the year of the black bean."

That year, the health department promoted the benefits of black beans, curiously the same year that farmers had a surplus. Black beans were introduced into school lunches with the promise of improving kids' health. Unfortunately, the results were disastrous. Musical farts that sounded like an orchestra interrupted every class in

the school. Some played a long note similar to a violin. Others let out a powerful bass sound. The most skilled students let out multi-pitched trumpet sounds that launched a competition.

Teachers quickly opened windows. Some had air fresheners. But nothing short of a tornado could overpower a class of middle school farts. Students left their classrooms to find a safe space, but there wasn't anywhere to go. Even the cockroaches complained and left the building. There was no choice, school had to be cancelled.

The next day, black beans were banned in school. Unfortunately, the idea for school sabotage had already been planted. Students got wind of the ban and planned to bring in other gaseous foods. They brought lentils, oat bran, broccoli, apples, and every wind-producing food that they could find. Farting power returned to Middle School 99. Students chanted the motto "If you pass gas, you can pass on going to class." And for a second day, classes were cancelled again. Some say this was the start of climate change.

A new solution was devised to address the pollution problem at Middle School 99. A gas tax was implemented. For every fart laid, a student would have to pay a dollar, or give one hour of community service. It was a great idea but had an issue of enforcement. Many kids would fart and quickly blame someone else to avoid the fine. Other kids used silent techniques, and the accusations became a huge source of conflict. There was a huge cloud of

suspicion. Despite the decrease in farting, the tax caused a huge increase in fighting.

The English department proposed that there should be a reward system for not farting and there should be an honor roll of paper for the highest achieving students. The English department called it "the student retention program" and came up with the motto "Just keep it in." Every student would wear a flower. If a student returned that flower fresh at the end of the day, he or she would receive free candy. If the flower wilted, the student wouldn't get anything. It was a great idea that made sense in theory, but when the program was implemented, kids figured out to steal other people's flowers or bring in extra flower from home in case they had to let a fart loose. The price of flowers went up around the neighborhood, and the fart problem remained.

Fortunately for Middle School 99, the fart problem destroyed so many clothes, that after a few months, farting became too costly. Unfortunately for Middle School 99, kids figured out other ways to pollute the air. Stink bombs were left in the hallway. Rotten eggs were left in trash cans. Shower-free weeks were planned. And finally, a family of skunks was invited into the front door. More school was cancelled in the year of the black bean than any other year in Middle School 99's history.

Today, you can still feel the effects of that foul stinking year. Whenever someone farts, teachers will try their best to ignore the horrible smell. They know what happens if kids realize the power of the fart. The whole is greater than the sum of its farts.

6

THE PIMPLE

All teenagers fear acne. Even a small pimple causes kids to lose sleep. But imagine the plight of Brandon, who had three huge pimples on his face. No matter what he did, they would not go away.

Ten years ago, there was a student named Brandon who was a seventh grader in Middle School 99. Brandon liked slapping people in the back of the neck, pushing people into doors, and tripping people's legs. If you got an answer right in class, he would call you a nerd. If you got an answer wrong, he would call you stupid. If you didn't say anything, he would call you weird. Brandon was

mean and had been the same way his entire life. And until the moment Jennifer transferred into class 722, he never ever had a pimple.

26

Jennifer recently moved from Colorado and was new to Middle School 99. Jennifer sat right in front of Brandon, and it didn't take long for Brandon to introduce himself. He started with a spit ball to her neck. He followed it up with a paper ball to the head. And he finished his introduction with a loud announcement declaring Jennifer's wardrobe was from the Salvation Army. But Brandon did not notice that she was wearing all black, and as skilled as he was in making others miserable, he did not make the connection that she might be a witch. When she stood up and announced, "What goes around comes around," he definitely didn't take her seriously. But he should have.

The next day, Brandon walked into school with a huge pimple on his nose. It was hideous. This pimple was so big, it made it look like he had a second nose—with snow on top. No one could look at him without laughing. Even when people were not looking at him, they were still laughing. Brandon tried to hide it with a Band-Aid, but the pimple would just push out the side, creating a big stage on Brandon's nose. Ms. Orton couldn't teach class with all the laughter, so he sent Brandon down to the nurse. He stayed there until school ended and snuck out a side door at dismissal before anyone could see him. Unfortunately for Brandon, his nightmare just started. He returned to class the next day with two pimples on his nose. Neither of them was small, and he looked like he had camel humps along the bridge of his nose. No one felt sorry for him. They either laughed at him or said, "What goes around comes around." He sought refuge with the dean, but even the adults could not look at him straight. A security officer figured out to put a bag over his head and cut out holes for his eyes, nose, and mouth. His pimples barely fit, but at least he could return to class.

On the third day, you guessed it: he had three pimples. If you think the situation could not have gotten worse, you obviously were not there that day. His third pimple was so large and heavy, Brandon had a hard time keeping his head up. It emerged from between his eyebrows, and it made him look like a unicorn. Everyone looked at Jennifer, who wore all black for a third straight day, for an explanation. Jennifer smiled and repeated what was considered a spell by some people and a curse by others, "What goes around comes around." Brandon wanted to take revenge by stabbing students with his horn, but he was afraid the puss would explode. He had to put a paper bag over his head again, but this time, he needed a special hole for his third pimple.

No one ever found out what happened on the fourth day because Brandon never showed up to school again. It has been debated for ten years whether his pimples were a coincidence or sorcery. But what cannot be debated is the meaning of the whispers you can hear in the hallway whenever someone is bullied. "What goes around comes around." And when someone comes to school with a pimple, everyone knows why.

7

INSINCERE DAY

Ms. Bryant, the assistant principal, was nostalgic about life in the olden days. She said life was good when kids were polite, kept their thoughts to themselves, and did what they were told. Her students complained that these kids in the olden days weren't being sincere. Ms. Bryant said, "Maybe being insincere is a good thing." And unfortunately for Middle School 99, Insincere Day was created as an imperfect antidote to impolite children.

"Thank you for this homework assignment. It is clearly going to make a difference in my life, and I can rest when I am dead." Julia's response to Mr. Torres's homework was an insincere remark on Insincere Day. "I really wanted your opinion on my dress, so I can join your clique, make everyone else happy, and have less people talking behind my back." Rebecca's remark was one of many negative comments on Insincere Day. "Can you talk louder, so everyone can hear about the amazing day of your pet mouse?" John's insincere question started a sincere fist fight and called into question the value of insincerity.

Ms. Bryant heard about the fight and knew she had made a mistake. Fortunately, she was experienced in correcting mistakes. She once ran out of gas, so she drove in reverse. She once arrived to school late, so she left early. One evening, she left the school lights on overnight. To fix it, she decided no one could use the lights during the next day. With this in mind, she declared that Insincere Day would be replaced by Truth Day.

Truth Day confirmed rumors about the teachers that have been circulating for months. Math teachers admitted that the kids would never need to know anything they were learning for the rest of their lives. Mr. Jones admitted that he was an alien in a human body because he committed an interplanetary crime. His admission of truth proved the rumor that he really was crazy. Truth Day also encouraged Jimmy to admit that eight of his ten girlfriends across South America were a lie, Sandy to admit her real name was Sparticalista, and Jennifer to admit she planted a rumor in Yesenia's backyard because she was jealous.

Also Oscar admitted that he always blamed other people when he farted.

Truth Day also caused problems. Teachers started admitting who were their favorite students and whom they hated. Students said the same truth to teachers. Secret love crushes were revealed on a massive scale and caused uncontrolled jealousy. Bottled-up anger and bitterness led 99 percent of all the conversations to start with the phrase "This is why I have always hated you." Matthew also told himself his own truth that he was the best-looking boy in the school, which annoyed everyone. Truth Day caused a lot of problems, but nothing Ms. Bryant couldn't fix.

Ms. Bryant substituted Exaggeration Day for Truth Day. For many students, this day was nothing new since they exaggerate all the time. For others, it was a chance to express their figurative side. Jerry said, "This morning, my pancakes spun around the kitchen, took the syrup and strawberries hostage, and escaped fearlessly to my mouth." Carlos shared his perilous journey to school, "Four pigeons attempted to bomb my path with bio hazardous weapons of destruction, but I escaped to freedom on my private rocket, also known as my skateboard."

The quality of poetry improved on Exaggeration Day, but unfortunately, conflicts became more dramatic. When Roger was accidently bumped in the locker room, he reported, "Sean catapulted me across the room, stole my inheritance, and gave me nightmares in my daydreams." When Sierra received a seventy-five on a test, she protested, "Mr. Peters destroyed my self-esteem, rigged the test because he hates me, and relegated me to a life as snowflake counter in Iceland." When Bryce came twenty minutes late to class, he argued, "I drank gallons of water to purify my body from the negativity in the school, and I needed a little extra time in the bathroom." Ms. Bryant recognized the problem and had the perfect solution. Kids needed to be more literal.

There was definitely more order on Literal Day. However, some aspects of the day were a bit disorderly. All the students wrote the words "Name" and "Date" when they were told to write name and date on their heading. Half the soccer team looked upward all day because their coach told them to keep their chin up. The other half were looking for dessert because they were told their next match would be a piece of cake. The theater club was a disaster because everyone was trying to break their legs. And the entire seventh grade answered, "The bottom of the page" when they were asked where the Declaration of Independence was signed.

At this point, all Ms. Bryant wanted was a normal day. She was tempted to declare a celebratory Normal Day, but that wouldn't be normal, right? Wouldn't there be a fight about the meaning of "normal"? No, she finally learned her lesson. Every attempt to get middle school kids to act a certain way backfires. That's why theme days don't exist anymore. And by the way, if you ever have a problem that grows into new problems, remember Ms. Bryant. Sometimes, it's just better to accept things as they are.

8

THE ITCH TO SNITCH AND
THE WEARY WITCH

Thirty-five years ago, Ms. Johnston could not get her English students to admit to anything they did wrong. Students claimed a cosmic coincidence when fifteen of them submitted the same literary essay. When a textbook was defaced with cartoons, everyone agreed that textbooks were not Disney job applications, but no one confessed. When Ms. Johnston asked about who was talking behind her back, students claimed amnesia, hearing loss, or the possibility of a very lonely ghost.

Behind the student silence was the recent transfer student Jacqueline. She rented pens by the minute and would create demand by stealing people's pens when they were not looking. No one said anything. She was behind her entire class denying that there was ever a homework assignment due Thursday. No one told the truth, and everyone paid the no-homework tax. Student silence was good business for Jacqueline but bad for Ms. Johnston.

Ms. Johnston thought about how to get more cooperation around cheating. She offered a free book, a free poem, and even free vocabulary words, but only Jacqueline offered free pass for no homework. Ms. Johnston offered a positive phone call home, but Jacqueline offered phone calls from the cool kids. Ms. Johnston offered extra credit, but Jacqueline offered street cred, which was the best credibility for a middle school student.

With no other choice, Ms. Johnston resorted to witchcraft. She needed Mr. Doherty, the resident witch of Middle School 99. He lived at the back corner of the teacher's lounge inside a locked closet that can only be opened at midnight. Ms. Johnston waited in the teacher's lounge after school hours desperately hoping for a solution to her problems.

At midnight, Ms. Johnston opened the door, and Mr. Doherty appeared. He seemed weary, probably because he had heard so many ridiculous spell requests for so many years. He was once asked for a spell to help make kids remember the date for the War of 1812. He was asked for a spell to help kids remember the length of the Hundred Years' War. One teacher asked for a spell for kids to remember the color of the White House. Sometimes, the spell requests were impossible; like making math interesting.

The worst spell requests came from teachers who would never really want what they asked for. He remembered a spell request from last year that resulted in a sudden transfer to Middle School 99: Jacqueline's transfer! A teacher asked Mr. Doherty for help so that students would handle their own problems, and the next day, Jacqueline took over the power in the classroom. He warned Ms. Johnston to be careful with magic because you get what you wish for, but Ms. Johnston was determined. And so the spell was cast.

The next day, Ms. Johnston arrived to school an hour early with her favorite book and coffee, awaiting a day free of trouble. Surprisingly, Jacqueline was waiting for her on the sidewalk and wanted to talk about something. Ms. Johnston could not believe the spell worked so fast! Ms. Johnston also could not wait to find out who was stealing her pens. Turns out though, Jacqueline didn't have a confession, she had a proposal. Jacqueline would give Ms. Johnston a list of every wrongdoing that ever occurred in her class in exchange for an unnamed favor in the future. Ms. Johnston agreed to the proposal and looked up at the sky to thank Mr. Doherty but then remembered he was in the closet.

When Ms. Johnston arrived at her room, there were forty-five confession letters, sixty-two apology letters, and a line of twenty-three kids who were desperate to report what they saw.

Her first period class had plenty of participation, but all the kids were overwhelmed with the itch to snitch. Roger was sneaking jelly beans into his mouth, the other students would battle over who could tell the teacher first. When Daquan had a number-three pencil, all of his classmates would stand on their chairs and hold up three fingers. When Georgia asked to copy someone's homework, hidden tape recorders would be used to bring her to school court. Middle School 99 had spies everywhere, and every broken rule caused a frenzy of tattle tellers.

That day left Ms. Johnston more exhausted than any other day in her teaching career. That night, she made a return trip to Mr. Doherty. She desperately asked him to cast a spell to cancel the first spell. Mr. Doherty shook his head in disapproval and couldn't believe another teacher changed their mind about what the initial request. Nevertheless, he cast a cancellation spell, and that is why kids are confused by the itch to snitch today. Sometimes teachers want kids to snitch, and other times they just want to be left alone.

Ms. Johnston? She had one last problem. Jacqueline was waiting for her outside of school after Mr. Doherty casted the cancellation spell. She requested the favor that Ms. Johnston had promised her. Jacqueline received more power than she ever had before. And Ms. Johnston was never seen again.

PART II

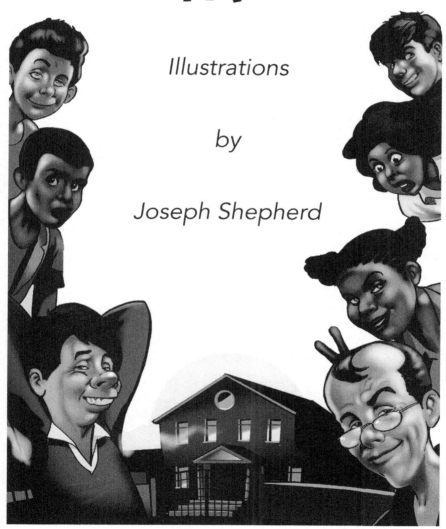

Illustrations

by

Joseph Shepherd

9

THE TWO LIARS

Every kid lies a little bit, and some kids lie a lot, but nobody lies like this boy, Jefferson. He lied for no reason, he lied for bad reasons, and he lied about lying. He was a student thirteen years ago at Middle School 99, and while he waited for class to start one day, he sat against a wall with a fork in his hand. As the class started, Jefferson found his attention drifting to the electric socket. He wondered, "What would happen if I stick a fork in it?" Well, he found out, and actually, everyone found out!

Crack! Bang! Zap! Everybody was jolted out of their seats. The lights flickered, and Jefferson's hair stood up on his head. Even his fork was burnt. As everyone looked at him astonished, Jefferson said, "It wasn't me."

Jefferson experienced no shame when he lied, and actually enjoyed the looks of shock every time he denied the truth. "You never told me the homework" was enough to have Ms. Walters cross her eyeballs and made her just a bit dizzy. "He hit me first" made Mr. Stern jump up in down in disbelief, causing him to lose his breath, which he actually never found again. "I never said that" created just enough doubt in Ms. Paulino's head that she started regular therapy. Jefferson thought that lying worked and was a great choice for entertainment in school.

Students weren't the only liars. Teachers lied too. "You might need to know this one day" is a terrible untruth. Another lie is "If you cheat, you are only cheating yourself." But how can teachers say this when they cheat on their taxes, lie about their age, and break their diets? And in every teaching manual is the most famous lie: "This will go on your permanent record!"

Mr. Henderson, a social studies teacher at Middle School 99, lied even more than the average teacher. Mr. Henderson taught that Australians discovered America, and that's why we speak English. He also taught that the idea of the three branches of government was inspired from a bonsai tree. He only kept his job because he helped kids learn not to believe everything they heard.

Jefferson's seventh grade social studies teacher was Mr. Henderson. It was surprising to no one that the first day they met, Jefferson lied about why he was late. Equally unsurprising, Mr. Henderson lied about the punishment for being late. This confused Jefferson, but he lied when he said he understood. Mr. Henderson lied that he cared. Wow! The battle of the liars began.

On the second day of school, Jefferson said he did his homework but left it home. Mr. Henderson lied that he would go to Jefferson's house during lunch to pick up his homework. Jefferson lied and said no one was home. Mr. Henderson asked for Jefferson's keys. Jefferson declared the right to privacy, without knowing anything about the constitution. Mr. Henderson said that kids do not have the same privacy protection as adults, also without knowing anything about the constitution. Everyone in the class left with neck pain that day, as the lies were thrown back and forth like a tennis match.

On the third day, Jefferson told a joke about a boy's mother getting fired from the M&M factory for spelling mistakes. When Mr. Henderson told Jefferson to stop talking, Jefferson lied that he was only talking to himself. Mr. Henderson lied that talking to yourself was a sign of insanity. Jefferson lied that Mr. Henderson called him insane and was going to report him to the principal. Mr. Henderson lied that he wasn't scared.

On the seventh day, Jefferson threw Mr. Henderson a curve ball. He told him that he didn't have his homework, he didn't know any answers to the first quiz, and he did not need to go to the bathroom. Mr. Henderson had only heard Jefferson lie. Therefore, Mr. Henderson sent Jefferson to the bathroom, gave him credit for his homework, and gave him an automatic perfect score for his quiz.

On the thirteenth day, Mr. Henderson told an inspiring story about his lifelong passion for education and why he became a teacher. The next day, Jefferson brought in multiple Internet photos of Mr. Henderson's failed attempt to be a comedian, musician, and beautician. On the twentieth day, Jefferson shared stories about his gang affiliation and tough street life. The next day, Mr. Henderson brought in pictures of Jefferson babysitting, dog walking, and enjoying an ice-cream cone at a peace march.

They were both really bad liars, and they deserved each other.

When students were matched with a teacher for tutoring, no one was surprised that the liars were paired together. Both Jefferson and Mr. Henderson requested anyone as long as it wasn't each other. Since they were famous liars, no one took their requests seriously, and they became each other's first choice. In the first session, Jefferson lied about not needing help. Mr. Henderson lied that he wanted to help. Shockingly, it was in this moment that they realized that they could actually help each other. They had a plan.

Jefferson started telling everyone that Mr. Henderson was an incredible teacher that made a huge difference in his life. He marveled at Mr. Henderson's encouragement, passion for teaching, and motivational speeches. Mr. Henderson reputation started to change. At the same time, Mr. Henderson told everyone that Jefferson was a diamond in the rough, a true example about the power of change, and a model student who demonstrates the power of giving kids a second chance. Both of them finally received respect from their peers and other teachers. Meanwhile, they spent all of their tutoring time doing nothing, except admiring the power of their lies. And they were never caught.

So if you tell an obvious lie, and you can't tell it's a bad lie, that is Jefferson's and Mr. Henderson's fault. Their success encourages both teachers and students to lie in every way possible every time. If you keep lying, you will always keep your accusers off guard. And if you lie in conjunction with someone else, you just might make it to the top. Mr. Henderson and Jefferson did it, and they are still hanging out in tutoring, doing nothing, while saying they did everything.

10

DEAN DRAMA

Dean Drama terrified Middle School 99. When she slammed her fist on a desk, dents were made on almost every desk in the school. When she yelled at you, her voice carried through the loudspeakers, so everyone knew you did something wrong. When she demanded that you sit up in your seat, an invisible force pushed every butt back, chest forward, and chin up. When she walked the hallways, everyone felt a deep desire to confess their mistakes. Dean Drama clearly was getting supernatural help, and

that help was from her mother, who was also a dean and who had died twenty-seven years ago.

Dean Drama's mother was a dean in the hippie era of the 1960s. She was known to the entire Middle School 99 community as "Dean Mama" and had a very unusual disciplinary style. Kids received candy every morning for being on time. Her detention became parties that celebrated an opportunity to change. Everyone loved Dean Mama and felt that they could do nothing wrong in her eyes. The problem was that the kids were doing plenty of things wrong.

When Angela Johnson stole a copy of the math test, she was celebrated for problem solving. Two kids who were caught fighting became captains of the debate team. Graffiti writers were celebrated for their artwork. Consequently, Middle School 99 graduates felt there were no consequences and wound up committing more crime than any other graduates in school history. And Dean Mama's policies were the reason.

Timmy Tapers stole cars because driving helped him go to sleep at night. Nina Covington was involved in a kidnapping gang because she was lonely. Christina Stone stole all the money in a charity basket to buy a trip to Alaska to see penguins, and there are no penguins in Alaska. When the Middle School 99 graduates were brought in front of the judge for sentencing, each of them cited Dean Mama's famous phrase, "Bad is fun, so don't judge." The judge snarled Dean Mama's name under his breath and gave each of them the maximum sentence.

Probably due to guilt, Dean Mama became sick and died before she had a chance to fix the problem. On her deathbed, her last wish was for her daughter to avenge her mother's name. Dean Mama wanted her daughter to be the fiercest dean in history in the most dramatic way possible, and this how Dean Drama received her name.

Dean Drama started her career with a meeting in the auditorium with all the students. Anyone who arrived late was handcuffed to a clock, including teachers. Anyone who squirmed in their seat was pinned down with

rubber bands. Anyone who asked to go to bathroom was given

a bus ticket to the next town. And if you even whispered, she would

51

blow a whistle in your ear until you promised to never open your mouth again. Discipline was immediately restored.

After the meeting, Dean Drama scattered all of Dean Mama's ashes throughout the school. Dean Mama's remorse and guilt were finally released. The ghost of Dean Mama showed her thanks by supernaturally helping her daughter. When a parent was called, the ghost of Dean Mama notified the entire extended family, including the dead. When a kid napped on their desk, the ghost of Dean Mama sent harrowing nightmares to awaken the child. And if the child received detention, he or she walked into the house of horrors and was never the same. Dean Mama did everything she should have done decades ago.

So if you think Dean Drama is ever being too dramatic, just remember that she is overreacting because of her mother's permissive mistakes. And if you feel an invisible force encouraging you, maybe forcing you to do the right thing, that's Dean Mama. And there is bad news for future students: Dean Drama is pregnant! Dean Trauma is on her way!

11

BEARS ON A FIELD TRIP

Eighteen years ago, a seventh-grade class at Middle School 99 went on a hike to the bear cave. Apparently there was a spot on top of a hill where bears used to live. The local forest ranger, Sam, tried to scare everyone with safety rules for confronting bears, but no one listened. The students had never seen a bear in the wild before and in fact, could only think fondly of their own teddy bears. Many of the students still slept with their teddy bears, and that's something that everyone kept a secret, except Javier.

Javier wore teddy bear pajamas to school. Javier had a teddy bear on his backpack. Javier ate teddy bear cookies for lunch every day. So imagine the excitement that Javier felt when Ms. Nuñez announced that the seventh grade was going on a hike to see the bear caves! He thought the universe merged his birthday, Christmas, and the nature channel into one day!

On the day of the hike, forest ranger Sam gave strict rules that everyone must stay on the path and stay close together. If they happen to see a bear, they were told to run away. It didn't matter how fast you ran, you just have to be sure you were faster than someone else. If there were two bears, they would have to run faster than two classmates. With this joke, everyone knew there were no bears around.

Javier hadn't given up hope. He knew that if he stayed on the path, he would never get to see his beloved bears. There were too many students on this hike, and any nearby bears would be scared away. He had to find a way to get by himself. As the seventh graders climbed a

particularly steep hill, Javier hid behind a tree, in which he thought nobody could see him. If he were a little skinnier, he might have had a chance at being incognito, but Javier ate a lot of teddy bear cookies, and his stomach would always betray him in a game of hide-and-seek. Fortunately for Javier, everyone thought he just needed to go to the bathroom, and they left him alone and kept walking.

Once he was solo, Javier immediately set out in a different direction. It didn't take long for him to be out of earshot of his classmates. He decided to wait in one spot until a bear crossed his path. He was wearing his Chicago Bears jacket and Chicago Cubs baseball cap, so he thought he just had to wait until a bear was attracted to his location. He also brought a bottle of honey as a backup plan.

As you can imagine, Javier waited for two hours without any sign of a bear. He became a little disillusioned and decided to return to his classmates. He walked back to the path and followed the tracks of the other classmates. He thought it was the worst trip ever. Javier had no idea what awaited him.

After thirty minutes, he arrived at the bear caves. The huge rocks were kind of cool, but the entrance into the cave seemed small, and it was weird that there was no noise. The tracks led into the caves, but there was no evidence that anyone was around. Javier thought that everyone must be playing a trick on him. So he entered the caves like someone who knew he was being thrown a surprise birthday party. The surprise couldn't have been any different than this.

Inside the cave, there was a large damp space with a fire in the middle. Around the fire were three bears. Well, actually, to say "bears" is really not accurate. These beings had human heads and the body of a bear. And they smelled badly too. The first bear said to Javier, "We have been waiting for you. Please sit down with us."

Javier sat down next to the bears, a little disconcerted at the situation but also puzzled. He asked, "Where is everybody? Where are my friends? Where are Ms. Nuñez and Sam?"

The second bear said to Javier, "We have been watching you for a very long time. It is time that you complete your initiation."

Javier was shocked by the stark tone and demand of the second bear and looked to the third bear for comfort. Javier said, "I am a little uncomfortable in this situation. If you were talking bears, everything would be fine. But the half-bear half-human thing, it's a little creepy."

The third bear nodded his head in agreement and said, "It definitely takes some getting used to. I'll tell you what. See that pile of meat over there? Eat the entire pile, and you will have proven your worth. We will show you out, and if you are lucky, we might even give you your bottle of honey back."

Javier noticed his bottle of honey was no longer in his pocket. These beasts were slick. He decided that eating his way out of this situation was his best choice. The pile of meat was near a wall and hard to see. It was a massive pile six feet high.

It was a daunting challenge, but he imagined that the pile of meat were teddy bear cookies, and after six hours of chomping, he finished his task. He turned to the bears and asked, "Can you escort me out now?"

The three bears laughed and pointed to the entrance. Javier scurried to the light and tried to get out but couldn't. He was suddenly too big. He looked down and realized that his body had transformed into the body of a bear. In that moment, he realized that he had completed his initiation. And he knew he would never return to the outside world. And he also knew why the bears smelled so badly.

So when a teacher tells you to stay together on a trip, well, just think of Javier. You might even hear him telling you to hide. I suggest you ignore those thoughts!

12

THE SCHOOL NURSE

Sixteen years ago, nobody wanted to go to the new nurse, Ms. Rogers. Students weren't afraid of her. She had a good medical reputation. Even her breath was only occasionally objectionable. Ms. Rogers's problem was she complained more than any other human in the universe.

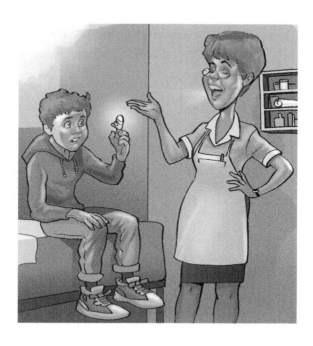

If it was sunny, she would complain about sunburns and the ozone layer. If it was raining, she would complain about kids falling on wet floors. If it was cloudy, she would be mad that Mother Nature couldn't make up her mind. She always found a way to be upset, and she loved to keep her audience captive. That was a problem for students because she had to sign the hallway pass to return to class. Many kids were stuck in that office until she ran out of things to complain about. You were lucky if she let you out at the end of the day. Some kids had to stay overnight!

Ms. Rogers also made you feel bad for any ailment you brought to her office. If you had a paper cut, she told you that you deserved it for cutting down a tree. If you had a sore throat, she explained that's what happens when you gossip. If you had a headache, well, she would start screaming at you for your demonic thoughts, which only made the headache worse.

Kids at Middle School 99 had to make a serious decision about when they were sick or hurt. Did you risk an overnight stay just because your stomach was in pain? Was your ankle sprain that bad that you were willing to hear Ms. Rogers's complaints about candy and soda? Almost everyone decided to avoid the nurse's office, and that resulted in Middle School 99 setting new health records. Visits to the nurse were down 83.975 percent that year! People came from all around the country to learn about the incredible improvement and advancement in school-based health.

You could think that the experts would have figured out the truth upon arriving at the school, but they misread the situation entirely. The experts concluded that Middle School 99 created an environment of powerful mental strength, a factory of grit, a paradise of strong will, where kids chose the hard path, to grind through difficulty, instead of seeking help. It was concluded that these kids were warriors and should be the leaders of tomorrow. The principal was promoted and was an educational star. Only late at night, when no one could hear her, would she admit the real reason that there was such amazing progress. It was the only change that made any sense. She started wearing vibrant green colors on Tuesdays and strong earth tones on alternate Fridays. She slept well knowing she helped children.

Nurse Rogers decided to stay in school, despite getting many offers to go on a speaking tour. She was afraid that if she didn't have a captive audience, people wouldn't listen to her complaints, would leave, and would want their money back. At school, the kids were helpless listeners, and because they were so sick from lack of medical attention, they were too weak to leave anyway. They were the best audience.

But this is where the story gets tragic. At the end of the year, one student had a contagious disease that got worse and worse and spread to others because of lack of medical attention. No matter how depleted he felt, he never sought any help. He was afraid of Ms. Rogers. Unfortunately the disease spread to five kids. And, more unfortunately, these five kids were also afraid of going to the nurse. A week later, fifty kids were violently ill—so badly, that they couldn't leave school. There weren't enough ambulances to bring them to the hospital. Those kids infected everyone else in the school. And the results were bad. The school had to shut down for three months, and most students were sent to isolation chambers. It took three years for life to return to normal.

The good news is that every disease-ridden child overcame the disease and eventually returned to school. The bad news is that the teachers immediately gave them five boxes of missing homework to complete if they ever wanted to return to their appropriate grade.

The other bad news is about Ms. Rogers. She disappeared and was never found. Even worse, there is a rumor that she substitutes in disguise whenever a school nurse takes a day off. So be careful if you go to the nurse,

and your familiar friendly face is not there. You might get stuck with the nurse who caused one of the biggest health problems our country has ever known. And you might also have to listen to her complain all night long.

13

THE WORST KIND OF GHOST

Do you hear a clinking or tapping sound coming from the radiator? Maybe you hear it coming from the pipes in the ceiling. You might even hear it from the air conditioner. Do not let anyone fool you, someone is making those noises, he won't stop, and his name is George.

Eighteen years ago, George could not stop tapping. He tapped his pen, and he tapped his foot. He even loved tapioca pudding. But nobody knew the real reason George was tapping until it was too late.

When George's classmate Sarah read a story about choking on a lifesaver, George was tapping the front of his chair. When Pierre was answering a math question, George was making percussive sounds in his mouth. When the class was interrupted by an announcement on the loudspeaker about not interrupting, George was slapping his shoulder and looking bothered by something behind him.

Nobody understood why George tapped all the time. However, one teacher was going to try to find out. Mr. Matthews asked George about his interesting habit in the hallway one day. George immediately started tapping his ear. At first, Mr. Matthews thought George was disrespecting him, but when George never stopped tapping, Mr. Matthews thought that the gesture was now an attempt to share a secret. So Mr. Matthews slowly leaned forward, head turned sideways to demonstrate he was listening. However, every time Mr. Matthews inched forward, George inched away. Mr. Matthews thought George was leading him somewhere, but George was just trying to retreat slowly without being rude. Over the course of seven minutes, they moved like an inchworm down the hallway into the doorway of the gym. Everyone looked at them curiously, but since they moved so slowly, it was actually kind of boring.

Eventually George backed into the door and entered the gym. Mr. Matthews thought it was odd that George was leading him into wrestling practice, and George thought that Mr. Matthews had an odd way of getting people to sign up for the wrestling team. Neither of them wanted to be there, but their discomfort was nothing compared to the wrestling coach. The wrestling coach was a behemoth of a man and was rumored to be cousin of Big Foot, Paul Bunyan, and Hulk Hogan. He also had a short fuse, some say due to his service in the United States's last six wars. Everyone called him Tank, and no one knew his actual name. Tank immediately grabbed

George in a headlock, and for the first time in George's life, he couldn't tap his body. George pleaded for Tank to let him go, but Tank mistook George for the enemy, and there was no letting go. And then the whole building shook. Twice. And then it was too late. George said, "You have no idea what you just unleashed." Tank looked around and realized he made the biggest mistake of his life. He let loose the most powerful, ghastly ghosts known to any middle school ever: gossip ghosts.

Up until that moment, gossip ghosts were constantly seeking to cause trouble, but George's tapping distracted the ghosts and they were contained in the pipes. But without George tapping, the gossip ghosts had nothing to distract them, and havoc ensued. Suddenly everyone knew who was talking about him or her, what they said, and whose boyfriend or girlfriend they were trying to steal. Immediately everyone's secrets, insecurities, and biggest fears were revealed. And if that were not enough, rumors and lies were spread to make everyone seem like a repulsive outsider, a villainous traitor, and a contagious disease. Yes, the gossip ghosts took over Middle School 99, and the one person who could control them couldn't anymore. He was in a headlock.

The gossip ghosts caused chaos. Melinda's boyfriend, Jack, was cheating on her with Noriya with the help of John and his sister Daniella. However, if Melinda admitted she used John to get back at Daniella, Jack would break up with Noriya. Joseph's cousin wanted to fight Jacob's younger brother after school when he was told a lie that his cookies were stolen and were sold for half price in the lunchroom. A rumor about Vicky telling false rumors made five other girls make up rumors against Vicky. Yes, it was a typical middle school day, on steroids.

After some struggle, Tank had to release George. Tank was mortified because the ghosts let everyone know that Tank never won a real wrestling match because he couldn't fit in a uniform. To his eternal chagrin, he could not put the howling ghost, his new target, into a headlock.

Once George was free, he knew he had to do something fast, and do it in a place that reached every part of the school. With the help of guilty-conscious Mr. Matthews, he ran to the boiler room to tap the pipes as loud as he could for as long as he could. The sound would reverberate throughout all the pipes in the building, and he hoped that this would be loud enough to scare the ghosts away.

When he reached the basement, George grabbed the custodian's broom and swung passionately and fervently on the pipes until the tapping could be heard everywhere. It worked! Every gossip ghost was mesmerized, followed the sound back into the pipes, and disappeared. Order was restored. Fortunately when the ghosts were gone, everyone forgot about the chaos and wondered only why their clothes were ruffled, bodies bruised, and egos checked. Unfortunately, George knew he had to stay by the boiler for the rest of his life. He had to protect the school. George is actually still there right now protecting you from gossip.

So when you hear a tap or clinking sound in the pipes, please thank George for his service. And if you feel compelled to gossip, spread rumors, or create drama, it might mean George is taking a nap. If that happens, I suggest you start tapping immediately.

14

THE BOY WHO ALWAYS ESCAPED DETENTION

Ronny Hernon often received detention, but he never served a minute. He was a Middle School 99 legend. Ronny used traditional excuses his first two months at Middle School 99 to avoid detention. He claimed he needed to pick up his younger brother, even though he didn't have one. He claimed he had a doctor's, dentist, or dry cleaner's appointment. He claimed that he had work or he needed to look for work. Ronny also promised he would do his detention the following day, which is something he said earnestly every single day. His tactics worked for a while, until the teachers realized they should not believe a word he said.

The teachers decided they would post someone outside of his classroom to make sure he served his detention. Ronny had to become more creative. The first day, he planted a stink bomb in the hallway to create a distraction. The second day he pretended to be sick and spit up fake vomit in the trash can. The third day he wore a long-haired wig and a dress and walked out undetected.

The fourth day, Ronny walked with the teacher down the hallway and then used the oldest trick in the book. He asked, "Can I go to the bathroom?" Every day, he figured out how to outmaneuver the teachers, and the other students celebrated his success.

It was decided that Ronny would need two teachers to escort him to the detention room. The first pair of teachers included the basketball coach and the track coach. Ronny couldn't outrun them, but he could outsmart them. Ronny asked both women what they thought of the student poll over who was the best coach in the school. As the coaches argued, Ronny slipped away.

The teachers decided that Ronny's escorts needed to be more intelligent. Five social studies teachers were given the task of bringing Ronny to the detention room. However, Ronny simply had to ask the meaning of the constitution, and the loud debate was all he needed to slip away.

Up next, it was decided that math teachers would not be tricked because they were the most logical. But when Ronny started singing the alphabet song, none of the math teachers could focus, and he slipped away again.

It occurred to the teachers that it was truly impossible to bring Ronny to detention. Detention would have to be brought to Ronny. In his last class, all of the kids would be dismissed. And the gym teachers would stay with him. Ronny was surprised when the gym teachers were not distracted by his sports questions. They stood by the doors and refused to respond to anything he said. He noticed that they were wearing ear plugs and even turned their backs to him. It was too easy. Ronny climbed out the window to the sidewalk, and he was free again.

The last day is when Ronny truly became a timeless legend. The entire faculty and the principal went into Ronny's last class to make sure he served his detention. Ronny had to stand in the middle of the room while all the adults stood around him. Escape was impossible, except for Ronny. He lit a smoke bomb and the lights went out. When the smoke cleared and the lights returned, Ronny was gone.

Some say he dropped into a trap door. Others say he climbed a rope to the ceiling and hid above everyone's head. But to this day, we will never know because Ronny was never seen again. The only thing left was a joke that started, "How many teachers does it take to bring a Ronny to detention?"

15

THE MASTER CHEATER

Bonnie Bellows received perfect scores on all her Spanish tests. She didn't speak a word of Spanish. Ms. Perez, the Spanish teacher, ruled out telepathy and was determined to catch the best cheater Middle School 99 has ever known. In the middle of the midterm, Ms. Perez had Bonnie stand up and searched for a cheat sheet with the answers. She even searched for the answers written on Bonnie's hands and arms. Unfortunately for Ms. Perez, she didn't check between Bonnie's fingers.

For math tests, Bonnie had her friends use hand signals to share answers across the classroom. In social studies, she sat it the front of the classroom, so she had a classmate behind her trace the answers on her back. In English, she wore earmuffs with headphones hidden in the fur. In science, she had a more challenging situation. She sat in the back of the classroom by herself. Undeterred, she placed used gum on her assigned chair on the day of the test and disgustedly asked to change her seat, next to her best friend.

The one class that baffled her was gym. How could she pass the push-up test when she couldn't do a push-up? How could she do ten jumping jacks when her feet had never left the floor? How could she win the one-hundred-yard dash? She had a reputation to maintain, and she was out of ideas. In the bathroom by herself, she looked at the mirror and pleaded for help. To her immense shock, the mirror responded.

"You have come to the right place," said a voice from within the mirror. Bonnie saw that there was a room inside the mirror with a throne, and on that throne was a large cheetah, who apparently could talk. "Physical feats are all in the mind. Use your mind as you always do, and make me proud." Some people say she imagined the conversation, while others say that she was connected to the king spirit of cheaters. But what can't be argued are the results.

Bonnie approached her physical fitness tests with surprising confidence. For the push-ups test, she placed a large spring under her shirt so she would bounce off the ground. For jumping jacks, she ordered her friend Jack to jump ten times. For the one-hundred-yard dash, she set up fake poop behind the finish line so that that no one wanted to win. Bonnie walked to victory.

Bonnie wrote a book of all the best ways to cheat before she graduated. It is available for everyone to see. Just walk into the closest bathroom by yourself, look into a mirror, and ask for help. You will receive all the wisdom you need to bend the rules, deceive teachers, and achieve greatness. The book is sitting in front of the king of cheaters, and he gleefully awaits your arrival.

16

IT'S NOT MY FAULT

Is the smell from your armpit? Or is your friend's breath? Did you step in poop, or did the wind bring in something funky? Is it me, or can I blame this smell on someone else? These are life's deepest questions, and they started thirty-five years ago with a student at Middle School 99. He smelled worse than the bottom of a lunchroom garbage can, worse than an old teacher who didn't brush his teeth, and even worse than a boy's bathroom at the end of a day. Adam Acron could clear a room faster than the dismissal bell. During group work, his

whole team asked to go to the bathroom. Even the mice protested his entrance into a classroom. Adam smelled really badly, and what's worse, he didn't even know it. Adam wasn't exactly sure why people seem to dislike his presence, and he would never find out because no one could get close enough to tell him.

Sometimes people would leave notes for him about his hygiene, but he didn't take the odor accusations seriously. He thought his hate mail was peer editing assignments. He always returned the notes with corrected punctuation and red circles around spelling errors. He once found his book bag full of soap, but he thought the extra weight was encouragement to work out. He thought the posters on the wall about daily showers were a good idea but ignored the fact that his photo was on the poster with a red X through it.

Adam Acron could not take a hint, but he was not born this way. Actually, for most of his life, Adam thought he was the cause of everything! When he rolled over at night, he thought he made the sun rise in the morning. If he sneezed, he thought he was pollinating the flowers. When he ran, he thought he was spinning the earth. And when the world was quiet, he thought he was supposed to make a speech.

Adam's sense of importance was never a problem until he met Principal Larkin. Adam's test scores were extremely low and an embarrassment to the school. He answered every question with his own name. What was the cause of World War I? Adam Acron. Why did Romeo kill himself? Adam Acron. What's the square root of sixteen? You guessed it—Adam Acron. The only time he ever answered a question correctly is when he was asked for his name.

Principal Larkin had a problem on her hands, and she knew there was only one solution: sorcery. Late at night, she reached into the hidden compartment of her

secret drawer and pulled out a magical small box that was only used in emergencies. Principal Larkin opened the box while chanting Adam's name, and a curse was created especially for Adam. He would never think he was the cause or reason for anything that happened for the rest of his life.

Adam now had a new problem. He wasn't responsible for anything. When he lost his pencil, he blamed everyone. When he found it in his pocket, he demanded to know who put it there. Adam also blamed the teachers for his poor grades. If they taught better, he would do better. Worst of all, Adam didn't think he needed to bath because according to him, he never smelled. Other people clearly disliked toothpaste and soap. It was never him.

Principal Larkin now had two problems. Adam's grades were terrible again, and other students could not concentrate in his presence. Adam had to receive a new schedule. He received tutoring from the mop in the broom closet first period. He received counseling from a flagpole second period. He did astronomy on the roof third period. And when everyone went outside, he practiced reading out loud in the empty auditorium. Adam's schedule kept him away from everyone and everyone away from Adam. Whenever he requested a change from the main office, he would find only empty chairs and signs that said "Out for lunch." It was easy to avoid a smell that penetrated through doors and pushed back walls.

It is assumed that Adam still keeps this schedule because he was never told to do anything different. He was never seen again, but people know he still is around because sometimes it smells for no reason. But be careful! Sometimes you might think it's Adam and it might be you. You too might get a very special schedule, and then you would know that you too were a victim of Principal Larkin's curse. You will probably even see Adam fifth period.

17

THE NINE WORST GUIDANCE COUNSELORS EVER

Thirty-one years ago, the most beloved guidance counselor in Middle School 99 retired. Her name was Ms. Nuñez, and her celebratory assembly included speeches from some of the thousands of students she helped. Stories were told about her unique ability to say just the right thing at just the right time and for creating a home away from home for anyone who felt lost in life. Unfortunately, her replacements were not only bad, they were the worst guidance counselors in Middle School 99's history.

Mr. Grayson was hired in September. He believed children needed an advocate, someone on their side. When one student received a sixty on a test, he admonished the teacher for not teaching the other 40 percent of the curriculum. When students got into fights, he gave them boxing lessons to defend themselves. When students were kicked out of class, he would help them make protest signs and march with them through the hallways. Mr. Grayson was fired.

Ms. Paulino was hired in October after she retired as a sergeant in the army. Kids would enter her office crying about what other kids were saying about them. Those same kids would flee five minutes later when they heard what Ms. Paulino had said about them. She commanded twenty push-ups if you complained about your feelings, and she demanded fifty sit-ups if you said you were tired. "Be tough" was her answer to every problem, and she loved sharing bloody war stories for motivation. She was fired but not before setting a new trend for wearing camouflage pants to school.

Ms. Addison was hired in November to be more empathetic. When there was a conflict between two students, she successfully listened passionately to whoever talked to her first. But you had to be first. If you talked to her second, she never believed your story and would blame you for the problem. The consequence was that whenever there was a fight, there was a second fight to see who could reach Ms. Addison's office first. She was fired for being biased and later received a job on cable news.

Mr. Tanser was hired in December to bring fairness to the job. He was a former detective for the police department. He successfully used his analytical skills to determine who stole Izzy's pen, who started the rumor about Michelle being fake, and why Matias felt lost. The problem was that his interrogation technique spilled over into counseling sessions.

"Where were you on the night of December third when you say felt depressed at home," he inquired while

shining a light into Pierre's eyes. "You are covering up other emotions," he speculated as he handcuffed Donovan to the table. "You say you feel alone, but I am right here, contradicting your story!" he concluded, as he looked to the one-way mirror, which was really just a normal mirror. Mr. Tanser was fired and received a job in the juvenile courts.

In January, Mr. Polski was hired to bring tranquility to the job. When Georgia complained about girls being treated differently than boys by teachers, Mr. Polski told her to breathe deeply, assured her that everything would be okay, and that problems were a part of life. When Arshad complained about the racial stereotypes he faced daily, Mr. Polski assured him calmly that facing insults is a part of growing up and that the best response to ignorance is to ignore it. When Glen was questioning his gender identity, Mr. Polski shared his own search to find his driver's license, which had been missing since Tuesday. Mr. Polski was fired and later became a New Age author and yoga/meditation instructor.

In February, Ms. Jones was hired right after receiving her certification, and she was told to be more sensitive to the students than previous replacements. She did listen to everyone and showed she understood by telling her own parallel stories of grief and difficulty. Ms. Jones left every day more relaxed after venting. Unfortunately, the students felt doubly troubled as they left school with their own problems and Ms. Jones's problems. Ms. Jones was fired and later received a job in public relations at a major corporation.

In March, Ms. Anderson arrived on a time-travelling mission. She learned in college that if kids could just think about the future, they could make the right decisions in the present. When Cassandra arrived to her office upset about her lack of friends, Ms. Anderson asked her to visualize her future as a poet. When Ricky asked for help with being bullied, she suggested he imagine himself as lawyer for social justice. When Billy wanted some advice for a career path for his future, her brain short circuited, and she was never seen again.

In April, Ms. Carlton expressed the worst counseling known to humanity: pity. "Oh, you poor thing" is how she responded to anyone's sad story. "Bless your heart" was the second layer of pretend sympathy that hid the fact that she didn't care at all and had nothing valuable to offer. "Sorry, we are out of time. You have to go back to class" was how she finished every conversation, and most of them were only five minutes. She was fired and later received a permanent job as an audience member on a morning talk show.

May, Mr. Apple was hired as the most accomplished and credentialed guidance counselor Middle School 99 has ever known. As a graduate of Harvard and author of three books, he would be able to provide the advice and guidance that the students deserved. The problem was the kids didn't understand anything Mr. Apple said. When Juan shared his dilemma about dating, Mr. Apple said, "The Freudian impulse manifested as a consequence of latent ambitions may result in transference and attachment disorder." Juan left the counseling session even more confused. Mr. Apple was fired and later wrote a book about the difficulty of being understood.

In June, there was a sign left on the door of the guidance counselor's office that read, "We give up." It stayed there until the beginning of next year, when a new hire was made, Ms. Nuñez's son. He promised to learn from the mistakes of the previous year and continue his mother's tradition of true compassion, understanding, and support. So if you currently are getting proper guidance, thank Mr. Nuñez for maintaining her mother's vision. If you are not, Middle School 99 might have hired a child from one of the worth nine guidance counselors in history. If the name matches, I suggest you leave immediately.

18

GRADUATION PRACTICE

Thirty-three years ago, Mr. Rosenbaum prepared the entire graduating class for a perfect graduation. The ceremony was in three days, and no one wanted any mistakes. He instructed the students during graduation practice: "Grab the diploma with the left hand, shake the principal's hand with the right hand, and whatever you do, do not trip on stage!" Mr. Rosenbaum gave a special warning to the girls who would be wearing high heels for the very first time. He said, "Many of you want to look great for your friends, for your family. So you will wear high heels, but many of you have never worn high heels in your life. Not a good idea! You will trip, you will fall, and you will be a Middle School 99 legend for all the wrong reasons!"

Unfortunately, this graduating class was overconfident. The basketball team won the league championship. The chess team came in second in the city. And one student was in a toothpaste commercial. They felt like they owned the world. Nobody was worried about tripping on the biggest day of their lives, and Rosita was dying to wear high heels!

On the day of graduation, Rosita took a few photos beforehand with her family and friends, but what she really was thinking about was being on stage. With everyone watching, she would have her diploma in one hand, shake the principal's hand with the other, and look down on everyone because she was wearing three-inch heels!

The ceremony was a little boring, but after a few bad speeches and a really long celebration from the basketball team, the principal called the names of the graduates. Rosita wobbled to the stage. Her ankles were so tired from practicing, she couldn't walk steadily. It was a bad look, but as long she didn't trip, she would be okay. As she approached the stairs, she saw a crack in the stairs. Due to her overconfidence, she didn't bother avoiding it. So you know what happened, right? As you guessed, her heel got stuck, and she tripped and fell.

Tripping is always embarrassing. It's even worse if everyone sees you. It's beyond worse if you trip at a bad time. And if you scream when you trip, the whole world stops and ends. And the scream she let out? It echoed all throughout the school.

The band stopped playing music. The line stopped. Even traffic stopped outside. Everyone looked at Rosita, but nobody knew what to do. And if the situation couldn't get any worse, the heel of her shoe was stuck in the crack.

Rosita, mortified, knew there was nothing she could do. She unstrapped her high-heel shoe, looked at Mr. Rosenbaum, feeling defeated, and had to take the photo with her diploma lopsided, because she was missing one shoe.

And that shoe was never removed from the stairs. It's still there now, left as a warning. And some people say, "When it's your turn to walk up the stairs, if you listen really carefully, you can hear Rosita's agonizing voice yell, 'Noooooooo!'" Some say she never stopped screaming.

DISCUSSION
QUESTIONS

1 • EIGHTH GRADE WILL BE THE BEST THREE YEARS OF YOUR LIFE

Have you ever failed in order to succeed?
Do you fear what will happen when you graduate? Why or why not?
Why do you think some kids misbehave?

2 • THE GIRL WHO LOVED CIRCLES

What is something that you are passionate about in your life that is considered peculiar by others?
What is something unusual that bothers you?
How does acceptance play a role in your life?

3 • THE BOY WHO CARED AND THE BOY WHO DIDN'T

How do you feel when you commit an act of kindness?
What is being cool and how does it affect people?
How can kindness be cool in your life?

4 • THE GRAFFITI WRITER

Can you change someone else's behavior?
Why is it important for some people to be known?
What's the difference between simply needing to be known and having a strategy to be known?

5 • THE GAS PROBLEM

What problems have you solved with good thinking?
What was a struggle in which it was difficult to find a
  solution?
In what situations have you experienced a solution to a
  problem that resulted in unintended consequences?

6 • THE PIMPLE

Does "what goes around come around"?
How do you handle bullying?
Did you feel sorry for Brandon?

7 • INSINCERE DAY

When is it important to say what you really think and
  when is it important to be quiet?
When do you exaggerate?
When has one problem turned into many problems?

8 • THE ITCH TO SNITCH AND THE WEARY WITCH

Why is snitching considered bad by some students?
When do you tell an adult? When do you keep it to
  yourself?
Who has the power in your class and why?

9 • THE TWO LIARS

Why do people lie?
What happens when people help each other lie?
When is lying a problem?

97

10 • DEAN DRAMA

What is effective discipline?
What is ineffective discipline?
What story about someone's past could explain his or her
current behavior?

11 • BEARS ON A FIELD TRIP

Have you ever gotten lost?
When in life is it dangerous to go off the path?
Why are ghost stories fun but also scary at the same time?

12 • THE SCHOOL NURSE

Who talks too much in your life?
How do you handle someone who complains all the time?
Who gets credit for something that he or she doesn't
deserve?

13 • THE WORST KIND OF GHOST

How has gossip been a problem in your life?
Why do you and other people gossip?
How do you handle gossip?

14 • THE BOY WHO ALWAYS ESCAPED DETENTION

What do you avoid?
What is your best escape story?
Does detention work?

15 • THE MASTER CHEATER

When have you cheated?
When have you thought outside the box to solve a
    problem?
Is cheating creative?

16 • IT'S NOT MY FAULT

Were you ever confused about whether you smelled?
Did you ever blame someone else for something you did?
How do you let someone know he or she smells bad?

17 • THE NINE WORST GUIDANCE COUNSELORS EVER

Who listens poorly in your life? What do they do?
Who listens well? What do they do?
What kind of listener are you?

18 • GRADUATION PRACTICE

When have you tried to look good but wound up having an
    embarrassing situation?
Does focusing on a fear make it worse?
How do you want to celebrate your graduation?

ABOUT THE AUTHOR

David Paris is an educator from New York City. He has spent twenty years teaching literacy, dance, and communication in the city's public-school system. At M.S. 88, Paris serves as a teacher, coordinator, and staff developer. He has led community- building workshops for teachers, students, and parents.

Paris is a tireless advocate for a literacy-based empathy curriculum. He is a nonviolent communication trainer with NYCNVC.org and a classroom teacher trainer for Outward Bound.

Paris is also passionate about acrobatic dance. He and his dance partner, Zoë Klein, were semifinalists on America's Got Talent. Paris has taught and performed in twenty-six countries and created nine instructional DVDs. His dream is to combine education with dance to teach a new generation of acrobatic performers.

Vist our website: www.MiddleSchoolLife.com

- Preview upcoming books and more laughable legends
- Free downloads for social emotional team building games and activities
- Join our Blog for an opportunity to create your own middle school stories

Made in the USA
Monee, IL
13 March 2022

92850824R00066